From the Chicken House

It's so exciting being part of a gang of friends, but I'm the only boy in the Chicken House girl gang, so sometimes I don't really know what's going on. They're always changing the codes without telling me!

I wish I was in Cornelia Funke's great story; I bet I could crack the mystery first!

Barry Cunningham
Publisher

Cornelia Funke

The SUMMER GANG

**Translated from the German
by Oliver Latsch**

Chicken House

2 Palmer Street, Frome, Somerset BA11 1DS
www.doublecluck.com

Text © Cecile Dressler Verlag GmbH & Co. 1993
English translation © Oliver Latsch 2011

First published in Germany as *Die Wilden Hühner* by Cecile Dressler Verlag
GmbH & Co. KG, Hamburg, 1993

Published in Great Britain in 2012
by the Chicken House
2 Palmer Street
Frome, Somerset BA11 1DS
United Kingdom
www.doublecluck.com

Cover illustration by Linzie Hunter
Cover and interior design by Steve Wells
Typeset by Dorchester Typesetting Group Ltd
Printed and bound by CPI Group (UK) Ltd, Croydon, CR0 4YY

The paper used in this Chicken House book is made from wood
grown in sustainable forests.

5 7 9 10 8 6 4

British Library Cataloguing in Publication data available.

ISBN 978-1-904442-86-8

For my parents

Chapter One

It was a wonderful day, as warm and soft as chicken feathers. Unfortunately, it was also a Monday, and the huge clock above the school entrance was already showing quarter past nine as Charlie came speeding into the school playground.

'Oh no,' she muttered as she shoved her bike into the rusty bike stand and yanked her school bag from the basket. She raced up the steps and through the empty assembly hall.

On the staircase she nearly ran over Mr Mower, the caretaker.

'Whoa!' he spluttered, nearly choking on his cheese sandwich.

'I'm sorry,' mumbled Charlie, as she rushed on. Two more corridors and she stood, panting, in front of her classroom. Behind the door there was a deadly silence, as always when Mrs Rose was teaching. Charlie took a deep breath, then she knocked and opened the door.

'Sorry, Mrs Rose,' she mumbled. 'I had to feed the chickens.'

Big Olly stared at her. Gorgeous Izzie arched her eyebrows, and Freddie, the class idiot, flapped his arms and crowed. Very funny.

'Well, that's an original excuse for a change,' said Mrs Rose, pursing her red lips as she put a cross in a little notebook.

Glum-faced, Charlie went to her seat. She stuck her tongue out at Fred and sat down next to Xa (short for Alexandra), her very best friend.

'You've got straw in your hair,' whispered Xa. 'Why did you have to feed the chickens? Is Grandma Slater sick?'

Charlie shook her head and yawned. 'Gone to her sister's. And now I have to get up an hour earlier every day to feed her chickens. A whole hour! Can you imagine?'

'That's quite enough whispering back there,' called Mrs Rose, as she began to draw mysterious sums on the blackboard. Xa and Charlie ducked their heads down until their noses nearly touched their books.

'But at least I had an idea,' whispered Charlie.

'Yeah?' Xa looked worried. Charlie's ideas were

generally worse than the flu. And she was constantly hatching new ones.

'Send a message to Hannah and Izzie,' Charlie hissed out of the corner of her mouth. 'Secret meeting, next break, girls' toilets.'

Hannah and Izzie sat next to each other, three rows in front. They were both studiously staring at the blackboard.

'Oh no,' groaned Xa. 'You're not starting with that being-a-proper-gang stuff again?'

'Write!' hissed Charlie.

Xa had mastered the gang's secret code perfectly, something that could definitely not be said of Charlie, even though she had invented it. Then again, she couldn't even remember how to spell 'teacher' – with 'ee' or 'ea'.

'Right,' said Mrs Rose. 'Can I have someone at the blackboard, please?'

Xa ducked. Charlie stared intently at her textbook.

'Any volunteers?'

'What's the password again?' whispered Xa, tearing a page from her exercise book.

Charlie scrawled something on the table. Xa screwed up her face. 'Huh? What's that supposed to be?'

'Duh. It's a chicken,' Charlie murmured. 'And it's the perfect password, OK? Hurry up!'

Mrs Rose was looking in their direction.

'Freddie's ready,' Charlie called out. She rubbed out the wonky chicken with her thumb.

'Ha, ha.' Freddie slid deeper into his seat.

'Done.' Xa carefully folded up the piece of paper and slid it across the table towards Charlie.

'Charlotte, how about you?' said Mrs Rose.

'Oh no, please, there's no point, really,' replied Charlie. 'Honestly there isn't, Mrs Rose.'

'Charlotte! To the front, *please*!' Mrs Rose's eyebrows were slowly knitting together. They always did this when she got angry.

Charlie stood up and walked to the front of the class. She snatched the note from her desk and dropped it into Izzie's lap. But hidden behind Mrs Rose's round glasses was a pair of eagle-sharp eyes. 'Isobel? Could I see that piece of paper?' Izzie's face turned crimson and she handed over Charlie's secret message.

'*Nekcihcdrowedockae rbtxenoolslrigehtnogniteem*,' Mrs Rose read out loud. 'What on earth's this?'

'That's Charlie's stupid secret code,' crowed Freddie. He was grinning so broadly that his ears were threatening to fall off. Charlie took a piece of chalk and stared at the blackboard, her lips pressed tightly together.

'Well, if it's secret,' Mrs Rose folded up Charlie's note and dropped it back into Izzie's hand, 'then it should remain secret. Charlotte, please begin.'

The rest of the lesson was pretty unpleasant for

Charlie, but at least her secret code had given Freddie something to puzzle over.

'This is a stupid place to meet!' declared Izzie. Three of them were squashed into a single toilet cubicle. Xa had the best spot. She was sitting on the lid.

'This is the only place where Fred's gang can't spy on us,' retorted Charlie.

'Spy on us? What's there to spy on?' said Izzie, playing with her blonde hair. 'I'm sure the boys have better things to do.'

'Really?'

Someone knocked on the cubicle door and whispered, 'Chicken. Chiiiickeeen.'

Charlie unlocked it and Hannah squeezed in to join them – now things were getting seriously cramped.

'Sorry,' mumbled Hannah sheepishly, 'but I had to go to the loo. For real, I mean.' She blushed. 'So, what's up?'

'Charlie's had an idea,' said Xa.

Izzie popped a piece of bubble gum between her white teeth. 'Well, if it's anything like the last one, count me out.'

'If being in a gang is such a waste of time why are you here?' Charlie muttered at her.

Izzie screwed up her eyes. 'Fine. Get on with it, then.' She giggled and gave Hannah a nudge. 'Maybe she wants to make another witch's potion – turn our faces green this time.'

Charlie replied with an icy stare.

'Please, do you think we could get to the point?' asked Xa. She climbed on top of the toilet and opened the window.

'All right.' Charlie rubbed her nose. She always did that when she was cross, or embarrassed. 'My gran's gone to visit her sister, who's even more ancient than her. I'm looking after the house for a week, and the chickens and all that. So, I thought it would make a brilliant hang-out, and if we meet a few times this week, well, we could maybe get to be a real gang.'

'I like it,' said Hannah, with a sideways glance at Izzie. For Hannah, a thing was only ever really OK once Izzie had agreed to it, but her friend wasn't looking at all convinced.

'What do you mean, a few times?' she asked.

'Like . . . maybe . . . every day?'

Xa shook her head. 'Oh, I'm not sure even I can make it that often. You know, my little brother . . .'

'Oh, you and your little brother again,' grumbled Charlie. 'Why can't your big brother look after him for a change?'

'What would you know?' mumbled Xa. Charlie had no brothers or sisters. Her mother drove a taxi, so she was hardly ever around. And her father, well, he wasn't around at all, and it was best not to mention him. Ever.

'And what are we going to do in this *gang*?' asked Izzie.

'Well, what do you usually get up to?' asked Charlie. 'Me, I just sit around at home, unless I'm slaving away at my gran's. Xa does nothing but look after her little brother. And Hannah's not exactly having one mega-adventure after another as far as I know, right?'

Hannah smiled awkwardly at the dirty tiles at her feet.

'Actually I have ballet,' replied Izzie smugly. 'And I have guitar lessons.'

'Wow, that's really exciting,' mocked Charlie. 'I'm sure you can't bear to miss those for one week.'

'Of course I can.' Izzie's eyes narrowed. 'But to do what?'

'Well . . . we'll see,' answered Charlie. 'You can't plan an adventure like a ballet lesson or something. They're there, *waiting*, around a corner, and then, suddenly, wham! – they happen.'

The other three looked at each other. Their heads were suddenly filled with exciting things. Charlie had done it again.

Hannah gave Izzie a tentative smile. 'I'd like to give it a try,' she said.

Izzie shrugged. 'Fine. One week. Then we'll see.'

Hannah beamed at her with relief.

'I'm in,' said Xa. 'I just might have to bring my brother.'

'Good.' Charlie took a deep breath. 'So we meet this afternoon, after school. Agreed?'

'Fine by me,' said Izzie. 'But I'm not putting on that stupid t-shirt again from before. It makes me look fat.'

'Well, we have to have something we all wear to show we're a gang,' replied Charlie. 'And I am definitely not getting into some strappy dress just to make you look good.'

'But wearing the same stuff is boring,' said Xa. 'How about a tattoo or something?'

Hannah's eyes almost popped out of her head.

'Just an idea,' muttered Xa.

'Maybe we can come up with something this afternoon,' said Charlie. 'And don't forget the password.'

'Chiiihiiicken,' warbled Izzie, rolling her eyes. 'And now can someone explain to me why we had to discuss all this in the loo?'

Chapter
Two

Charlie and Xa lived on the same street, which was handy when you were best friends. They'd known each other since nursery, had fallen out at least a hundred times, and had made up just as often – as best friends do. Once they had even run away together – all the way to the next street corner.

At four o'clock sharp, Charlie picked up Xa to go to her gran's. Xa was pushing a buggy because she had to look after her little brother Luke again.

'A baby!' Charlie shook her head. 'We're never going to be a proper gang.'

Whoosh! Out flew Luke's dummy from the buggy.

'Oh no!' Xa quickly snatched it from underneath a Chihuahua which was about to pee against a newspaper stand.

'Can't your big brother look after him for a change?' asked Charlie.

'No.' Xa carefully wiped the dummy on her t-shirt. 'He's got tennis.'

'Right. And last time it was what? Karate?'

Ping! The dummy went flying again – higher this time.

'Karate is Wednesdays,' said Xa. 'Oh no! Where's it gone now?'

Luke started screaming.

'Probably landed on the road and been flattened,' Charlie said impatiently. 'Haven't you got another one? He makes more noise than all the cars put together.'

Xa quickly pulled a clean dummy from her pocket and stuffed it into her brother's little mouth. When Luke had just been born Charlie had called him 'sugar-bear', but by now her enthusiasm for the baby had waned considerably. Xa felt the same.

They turned into a narrow street. After only a few steps the noise of the traffic faded to an angry rumble and they could hear the wheels of the buggy crunching on the gravel.

'So what do the boys do in their gang?' asked Xa.

'They go fishing,' replied Charlie. 'And they annoy girls. That's all those bird-brains can come up with.'

'What about us?' asked Xa. 'Have you got any ideas? Maybe we could cook together or something. Izzie would probably like that, too.'

'Izzie, Izzie, Izzie. She can go off to her ballet lessons if she starts whingeing!' Charlie shouted. Luke immediately started howling again.

'Keep it down!' hissed Xa. She quickly rocked the buggy until the baby had quietened down again.

'I'm sorry,' Charlie whispered. 'It just gets to me how Hannah worships her, and now you too. Anyway, cooking's not what gangs do.'

'It was only an idea,' replied Xa. 'Why did you let Izzie join in the first place if you hate her so much?'

'There was nobody else around,' muttered Charlie, rubbing her nose. 'And it was you who suggested her, wasn't it?'

'I thought of Hannah because she's always over at our place.' Xa's mum was very good friends with Hannah's.

Charlie sighed. 'And Hannah won't do anything without Izzie.'

'Exactly.'

Charlie hadn't suggested anyone else. Who could she have suggested, anyway? Xa wasn't just her best friend, she was her only friend.

'Doesn't matter,' continued Charlie. 'A gang is a gang, and those two are OK really. You'll see; this is going to be a great week.'

'I know,' replied Xa, although she didn't sound very

convinced. 'Could you have a peek in the buggy?'

'Fast asleep,' observed Charlie. 'Phew! Babies are so much cuter when they're sleeping!'

Charlie's grandma lived in a narrow street with meadows on one side and a row of old houses on the other. The houses were neither big nor pretty, but they all had big gardens.

Xa had only been there once before, and that had been enough. Grandma Slater didn't like it when Charlie brought friends over. 'I don't like strangers in my house,' she would say. And to her everybody was a stranger, except for Charlie and her mum. Grandma Slater was pretty strange herself. She kept forgetting things, and she enjoyed bossing people around. When Xa had met her she had suddenly understood why Charlie was often sad, and why she could be so nasty to others, sometimes even to her best friend.

When Charlie's mum was out driving her taxi, Charlie would eat at her gran's, and when her mother did nights Charlie had to sleep over. After tea she'd have to weed the garden for hours, or clean out the chicken coop. Grandma Slater was of the firm opinion that children should 'earn their keep'. 'By the sweat of their brow,' she would say. 'Yes, indeed, by the sweat of their brow.'

And so Charlie knew a great deal about vegetable

gardens and chicken coops – and mean old grand-
mothers.

Grandma Slater's house was the last one on the street –
a gloomy brick house with tiny windows that looked
like squinting eyes. There wasn't a patch of grass anywhere in the large garden, or a terrace, and there were
hardly any flowers. But there were countless berry
bushes and fruit trees, as well as long rows of tidy vegetable patches. At the back was an old shed and a green
henhouse with a large chicken-wire run in front of it.

'Oh, look at the hens!' exclaimed Xa, as they stopped
in front of Grandma Slater's gate. 'Are there any new
ones?'

Charlie shook her head. 'Nope. In fact, there's less.
Gran killed one last week to take to her sister's.'
Charlie's desperate pleas and even her tears had done
nothing to stop her grandmother. But at least she had
spared Charlie's favourite chicken.

'Oh no!' cried Charlie. She yanked the gate open
and ran towards the vegetable patches. 'Get out of
there! Shoo!' she yelled.

A fat brown hen peered out from between the cabbages, a large leaf still hanging from her beak. When
she saw Charlie charging towards her, she quickly
flapped over to the coop, clucking loudly.

'Just you wait!' muttered Charlie. She tried to grab

the hen, but the bird squawked in panic and ran up and down the fence. Charlie made another lunge for her. Feathers flew. Then the hen suddenly ducked her head, slipped underneath the green gate and back into the pen.

Xa was choking with laughter.

'Stop giggling, you idiot.' Charlie ran back to the cabbage patch, looking worried. Two of the cabbage heads had been reduced to stumps. She tugged them out of the ground and threw them down. Xa carried on pushing the buggy towards the house, still smiling.

'It's not funny,' cried Charlie after her. 'I'm going to be in big trouble when my gran sees this.'

'Come on, it can't be that bad,' replied Xa. 'Oops! Now I've got hiccups.'

'Those stupid birds keep digging under the gate,' Charlie sighed. 'I fill up one hole and the very next day they dig a new one. Try explaining that to my gran!'

'Calm down.' Xa put her arm around Charlie. 'If she's as forgetful as you always say then she'll have no idea how many cabbages she had in the first place.' She peered into the buggy. 'Luke's sleeping like a log. I'll just leave him here.'

Charlie still looked anxious. 'My gran never forgets about *that* sort of thing,' she said. 'She'd forget her own name first. She even knows how many rusty nails she's got in that jar in the shed.' Glum-faced, Charlie pulled a bunch of keys from her pocket. There were three gleaming security locks on Grandma Slater's rickety front door.

Xa stared in amazement. 'Has your gran got some sort of treasure in there?'

'Not as far as I know,' grumbled Charlie. She fiddled exasperatedly with the front-door keys. 'Gran sees burglars hiding behind every cabbage. There's nothing to steal in here. Come on.' She pushed the door open.

They walked through a small hallway, past a huge wardrobe, and went into Grandma Slater's kitchen. It was a beautiful kitchen. There was an old cupboard with lots of drawers and glass doors, and a big table with three chairs and a sofa.

'Looks comfy,' Xa commented. But Charlie was frowning again. 'Just look at that,' she muttered. She walked over to the cupboard and pulled off a note that had been taped to the glass front.

'"Monday and Wednesday: wipe floors",' she read. 'Charming, isn't she?'

There were more notes. They were everywhere: on the oven, on the fridge, on the door to the larder, even on the table. Sometimes there were two notes in the same place. All of them contained exact instructions. Charlie tore them all down, her face bright red.

Xa took the pile of instructions from her friend and started to read. 'Feed the chickens – clean the coop –

weed the vegetable patches (and do it properly this time!) – air the house – change the tablecloth – dust here, sweep there, wipe that . . .' Finally, Xa had read enough, and she threw the whole lot on the table.

There was one more note, taped to the tabletop. This one had an even bigger bunch of keys next to it.

'*Red:* key to the larder – fingers off the biscuits.

'*Blue:* shed. Make sure there's always fresh bacon in the mousetraps.

'*Yellow:* spare keys for front door – just in case you "mislay" yours again. Wouldn't be the first time.

'*Green:* letter box. Empty <u>daily.</u>

'*Black:* none of your business!'

'What's that supposed to mean?' Xa asked, perplexed. 'Maybe she's got treasure hidden here somewhere after all. What do you think?'

Charlie shook her head. 'No idea. It's a bit weird.' She looked hard at the black key. It didn't look any different from the others. 'Hey, Charlie! Are you in there?'

Someone called from outside, waking up Luke with a howl. 'Hello,' said Izzie, sauntering into the kitchen with Hannah in tow. 'You know, your baby's crying.'

'No wonder, with all the noise you're making,' growled Xa. She went out and got him. 'He's soaking wet. I've got to clean him up. Can someone put his changing mat on the table?'

Quick as a flash, Hannah rushed off to get it. But

while all this was going on, Charlie just stood there, staring at the black key.

'Out of my way,' grumbled Xa. She freed Luke from his soaking nappy with a mesmerised Hannah looking on.

'Hey, what's so interesting about that key?' Izzie asked Charlie.

'That's what I'd like to know,' said Charlie thoughtfully. Then she stuffed the keys and the pile of rude instructions into her pocket.

Chapter Three

'There are no cockerels,' observed Izzie.

The four girls were sitting in the middle of the chicken run, around a rickety table laid with tea and biscuits.

'Cockerels just cause trouble,' explained Charlie. The hens were squabbling over crumbs under the table. Charlie grabbed a small black hen and put her on her lap. She gently stroked her comb and the chicken closed her eyes.

Izzie giggled. 'Aren't you afraid she might poo?'

'No, but then I'm not as dressed up as you,' replied Charlie. Izzie pursed her lips and brushed the crumbs from her dress.

'Do they all have names?' asked Hannah.

Charlie nodded. 'Oh yes. This one is Emma, down

there are Isolde and Huberta, the speckled one is called Kokoschka, and those two fat ones are Dolly and Clara.'

'Nice names,' said Izzie. 'Did your gran come up with them?'

Charlie shook her head. 'No, I named them all. And our gang should have a name too, don't you think?'

'Freddie's gang has a great name,' said Xa. Luke was on her lap, dry and happy, and sucking on her finger.

'The *Piranhas*?' Charlie screwed up her eyes. 'You think that's great? I don't think so.'

'And they all have earrings.' Hannah stirred four spoonfuls of sugar into her tea. 'They all got into massive trouble with their parents for that.' Her admiration was obvious.

'How about,' Izzie took another of Grandma Slater's forbidden biscuits, 'we call ourselves the Pixies? Sounds good, I think.'

'Over my dead body!' Charlie lifted the kicking Emma from her lap and put her back under the table. Hannah was reaching for the biscuit tin again, but Charlie pushed her hand away and snapped the lid shut. 'That's enough, or my gran will know I couldn't have eaten them all myself.'

'Oh. Sorry.' Embarrassed, Hannah folded her hands in her lap.

'So come on, what's your suggestion then, Charlie?' sniffed Izzie.

'The C.H.I.X.,' answered Charlie. 'After the first letters of our names. What do you think?'

Izzie made a face. But Hannah and Xa were nodding.

'That sounds fun,' said Xa. 'Yes, it definitely sounds fun.'

'And for our look,' Hannah was excitedly shifting in her chair, 'we could all paint our fingernails green.'

'No, our toenails!' Xa chimed in. 'Or our lips!'

'Yuck!' moaned Charlie. 'Then we might as well all dye our hair.'

'No way!' shrieked Izzie, wiping at her shoe with a napkin. 'If you really want to call us the C.H.I.X., fine. But I'm not dyeing my hair!'

'I know!' Hannah blew her fringe out of her eyes. 'We could all wear a chicken feather around our neck, that we must never lose, or have taken from us, or else . . .'

'Umm . . .' Charlie was thinking.

Izzie grimaced. 'Ew! We'd all smell of chicken poo!'

'No, we wouldn't!' Charlie picked a feather from the ground and held it under Izzie's nose. 'Can your perfect little nose smell anything? Exactly!' She looked around. 'Everybody pick one. Plenty here to choose from.'

The chickens looked even more puzzled than usual as the four girls ran around their run, their eyes glued to the ground. It took a while for each of the C.H.I.X.

wild and exciting place. *It's her voice*, thought Xa. Charlie's voice was always a little raspy; it brushed against your skin like sandpaper.

'Come on, Charlie, don't go all mysterious on us,' said Izzie. She was always the first to break free of her spell.

But Charlie shook her head. 'Tomorrow . . .'

'Fine. I have to go home now anyway,' said Xa. 'Luke's getting hungry.' She walked over to the buggy.

'All right.' Izzie and Hannah got up as well. 'Yuck!' Izzie stared at her shoes. 'One of those stupid chickens has just pooed on my shoe!'

'They always choose the nicest ones,' Charlie giggled.

Izzie glared at her, then turned away. 'See you tomorrow then. Hannah, come on!'

'Bye, see you.' Hannah quickly ran after Izzie.

Xa was already by the gate, looking for Luke's dummy again. 'Aren't you coming?' she shouted over the fence to Charlie. Luke was now howling.

Charlie shook her head. 'I'll stay here for a while. Mum's still out driving anyway.'

Xa had found the dummy under the hedge. It had an old sweet wrapper stuck to it.

'Right then,' she said. 'See you tomorrow. Take care.' And off she went, pushing the buggy.

'See you,' replied Charlie. She put the cold tea

things on a tray and shook out the tablecloth before carefully checking it for stains. At least half of it was covered with mucky fingerprints. Why did Hannah have to eat all the time? Charlie took the tablecloth into the house and put it to soak. Then she took the table and the chairs back to the shed and looked around the garden. No. Not even Grandma Slater's sharp eyes would have spotted any signs of the first C.H.I.X. meeting.

Charlie took a handful of chicken feed and sat down on an upturned bucket in the middle of the run. The hens came strutting towards her. They pecked at her fingers, plucked at her shoelaces and blinked at her with their button-bright eyes.

Charlie had to laugh. Chickens were so funny. She took the keys and her grandmother's note from her pocket and looked at them again. The hens peered at her curiously and pecked at the piece of paper.

'How weird,' muttered Charlie, turning the black key over in her hands. 'Really weird.'

Then she fetched three eggs from the coop and pulled a few potatoes from the ground. Time for dinner.

Chapter Four

The next afternoon Xa didn't have baby duty and the girls had hardly any homework. It was the perfect time for another C.H.I.X. meeting.

At four o'clock sharp they all sat around Grandma Slater's kitchen table, waiting excitedly for Charlie to reveal her secret. The sun was shining through the open window; a magpie could be heard while bees were humming in the lime tree by the house.

Charlie cleared her throat and looked at their eager faces. She held out a few more seconds for maximum effect.

'Oh, just spit it out!' Izzie burst out.

'Yes, please do,' added Hannah, tucking into a sausage roll.

'Shall I make some tea?' asked Charlie.

'No,' said Xa, grinning. 'Just tell us!'

Charlie reached into her pocket and produced Grandma Slater's bunch of keys and the note. She put both on the table, a look of importance on her face. Then she read out a slightly shorter version of the note.

'Nice granny you have,' said Izzie after Charlie had finished.

'The secret is about the black key, isn't it?' asked Hannah, in a hushed voice, her eyes as round as coat buttons. For a moment she even forgot about her sausage roll.

'Last night, after you three left, I tried all the locks I could find,' Charlie told them. 'Nothing.'

'Do you think your gran has some sort of treasure hidden here somewhere?' whispered Hannah.

'Hannah, why are you whispering?' asked Izzie. 'Do you think Charlie's gran is hiding in the wardrobe or something?'

Hannah blushed and bit her lip.

'It's probably not treasure, but a horrible old corpse,' said Xa. 'Did your grandpa disappear suddenly?'

'Don't be silly!' Charlie shook her head crossly.

'Well, the way that note is written,' giggled Izzie, 'I'd expect something nasty.'

Outside, one of the hens started squawking madly. Charlie looked over at the window and frowned.

'Why do you think she's making such a big deal

about a key?' asked Xa. On the way home yesterday, she'd racked her brains over it, but had only succeeded in scaring herself about Charlie's gran.

'Maybe it's just the key to a drawer where your gran keeps her special cookie recipes,' suggested Izzie. But Charlie wasn't listening. She was still staring at the window. Suddenly she got up and crept towards it.

Hannah looked at her quizzically. 'Hey, what . . . ?'

Charlie had put a warning finger to her lips.

'So, maybe there's nothing mysterious at all about that key,' said Izzie, raising her voice deliberately. She'd also got up and was now tiptoeing towards the front door.

'Nah, definitely not,' agreed Xa, sneaking up to the window behind Charlie. Only Hannah was left sitting at the table, her mouth open with a half-eaten sausage roll in her hand.

Suddenly, Charlie screamed out: 'Spies!' and with that she jumped up on to the sill and out through the window. Xa followed, though not quite so quickly on her shorter legs. And Izzie tore open the front door and ran outside.

Hannah shook herself out of her daze. She struggled off the sofa and stumbled to the window, just in time to see Freddie, Tom, Olly and Will – the entire Piranha gang – running off across Grandma Slater's vegetable beds. Charlie, Xa and Izzie were hot on their heels.

They had nearly caught up with them when Charlie shrieked and pointed at the chicken run.

The gate was wide open. And the run was deserted.

It was Charlie's moment of shock that saved the boys. They climbed over the garden gate, grabbed their bicycles and sped off.

'The hens! They've all gone!' gasped Charlie. Her lower lip was trembling a little. She looked around, but the hens had vanished.

Panting, Hannah caught up with the rest of the girls. She stared at the empty pen. 'Maybe they're inside the henhouse?' she suggested.

Charlie shook her head.

'That's so mean of them,' said Xa. 'Really, really mean.'

'Come on.' Izzie took Charlie by the arm. 'Where's the chicken feed? Maybe we can tempt them back.'

'I see one, by the cabbages!' Xa called out. 'It's the speckled one.'

'Watch she doesn't run away,' shouted Charlie. 'We'll get the feed.'

'How am I supposed to do that?' Xa called back. But the others had already vanished into the shed. Xa crept around the hen so she could at least block her path to the gate. The hen's head shot up and her little eyes blinked nervously at the girl.

'It's all right, stay calm,' murmured Xa.

The hen clucked quietly.

The other three girls came out of the shed. Izzie and Hannah had handfuls of chicken feed. The hen turned towards them, though she took one last peck at the cabbage in front of her.

'Come on, Kokoschka, come,' said Charlie soothingly as she edged closer. Izzie threw some feed on to the ground in front of Charlie's feet.

'We have to surround her,' hissed Charlie. They spread out. Kokoschka craned her neck with interest.

'Crouch down,' whispered Charlie. 'So you won't seem so huge to her.'

'We'll never catch her!' moaned Izzie.

'Of course we will. Chickens aren't very bright. Throw her some more feed.'

Slowly, stretching her neck forward, the hen came closer. She kept a wary eye on the other girls. Xa tried hard not to giggle. Eventually, Kokoschka was pecking at the feed around Charlie's feet, and that was when Charlie grabbed her. She squawked in protest, kicked her red legs and jerked her neck left and right, but Charlie held on tight.

'One down,' she said, throwing Kokoschka over the fence into the pen, where the hen retreated huffily into a quiet corner. 'But where are the others?'

She looked around desperately. The other girls had never seen her so upset.

'Don't worry, we'll find them,' Xa tried to comfort her. 'They can't have gone far.'

'You don't understand!' cried Charlie. Her lip was trembling again. 'My gran'll kill me if even *one* of her hens is missing.'

'Come on, Charlie. Calm down,' said Izzie, patting her friend's arm. 'Nobody is going to kill anyone over a silly hen.'

Charlie pushed Izzie's hand away.

'Maybe not, but I'll never be allowed to come here again,' she snapped. 'Come on, let's keep looking.'

Deflated, the others followed her.

They found Huberta and Dolly in a lettuce patch belonging to Grandma Slater's neighbour on the left, and Emma and Clara in the high grass on the other side of the road. The neighbour screeched like a magpie about her tattered lettuces, and Emma got them into trouble with a car driver by landing on his windscreen. Only Isolde was nowhere to be seen.

Scratched, sweaty and tired, the C.H.I.X. finally gave up the search and returned to Grandma Slater's kitchen. The bunch of keys and the note were still lying in the middle of the table, but at that moment nobody was interested in mysteries.

'Just wait till I get hold of those boys,' muttered Charlie darkly.

Izzie looked at the kitchen clock. 'Oh no. As soon as I get my breath back, I've got to get home.'

'I don't understand,' said Hannah. 'How did they know we were meeting here today?'

'Maybe we have a traitor . . .' Charlie let her eyes wander over the three girls' hot faces. Her gaze fell on Izzie.

Izzie returned her stare angrily. 'What are you looking at me for? Maybe it was you who blabbed.'

The two of them glowered at each other across the table.

'I'm not the one who hangs around with boys all the time,' growled Charlie.

'We don't all hate boys as much as you do,' Izzie hissed back.

'Please, stop!' cried Hannah. She was close to tears.

'Yes, that's enough!' Xa banged the table. 'This traitor-talk is nonsense. The boys all know where Charlie's gran lives. They just had to follow one of us here. That's exactly the sort of thing they love doing. And Freddie's smart enough to have noticed that the four of us have started meeting up in the loo again.' She shot Charlie an angry look. 'It really isn't such a super-secret meeting place.'

Embarrassed, Charlie looked down at her scratched hands.

'Sorry, Izzie. I'm . . . I'm just a bit upset because

Isolde's gone.'

Izzie shrugged as she got up. 'Forget about it. I'm just tired! Shall we meet again tomorrow? We finish school early then.'

'If you'd like to,' murmured Charlie, ruefully. She was still looking down at her hands.

'Of course we'd like to,' smiled Izzie. 'We still have to solve the mystery of the black key. But now I really have to go.'

Chapter Five

Charlie found everything she needed in the garden shed – twine, a drill, an old window box and loads of empty tins. Grandma Slater always held on to her empty tins and jars. She used them to keep nails, buttons and other knick-knacks in. Charlie also spotted three mousetraps which her grandma had loaded with bacon just before her departure. Charlie let them all snap shut. Then she dragged the tins and everything else to the garden gate. There was still no sign of Isolde anywhere.

'Just you wait,' muttered Charlie, grabbing the drill to make some holes in the sides of the tins. She tried not to think of all the terrible things that might have happened to the hen, but that didn't work very well at all. She was sick with worry, and afraid of what her gran might say.

She placed the window box upside down behind the hedge, so that it couldn't be seen from the front gate. Next, she threaded the twine through the holes in the tins and lined them all up on the box. Then she tied the long end of the twine to the latch on the gate. She inspected her contraption, her face fierce. Yes, this would do the trick. As soon as anyone tried to open the gate the tins would fall off the window box, making a noise loud enough to be heard from inside the house. Charlie gave it a try, just to be on the safe side. It worked! Gran's ever-grumpy neighbour, Mr Stringer, peered over the hedge and barked: 'What's going on here?' And at least three dogs started howling. Well, if that didn't send a bunch of spying boys packing, nothing would.

Charlie carefully put the tins back on the window box. Then she ran over to the henhouse. The hens were already sitting inside on their perches, their eyes firmly closed and their feathers fluffed up. They just clucked sleepily when Charlie came in to check once more for eggs. Emma was sitting by the door with Kokoschka behind her, next to Huberta. Charlie was always amazed by how early chickens went to sleep. Grandma Slater had once explained to her that the weakest hen always sat right by the door, while the strongest sat in the middle. That was the warmest spot. On cold winter nights, each hen might even tuck her comb under the bottom of the one in front, so that it wouldn't freeze.

Usually it was Isolde who sat in the middle.

If Freddie or any one of those stupid Piranhas were here right now, Charlie thought, *I would kick their backsides so hard they wouldn't be able to sit down for days.*

There were three eggs in the nests, which weren't actually real nests but small wooden trays that were padded with straw, with a china egg in each to encourage the hens to lay.

Charlie carefully took out the eggs. 'Sleep tight,' she said. Then she quietly stepped outside and latched the door behind her. The henhouse had a small feed room where Charlie's gran kept the straw and food. Charlie put the eggs on the straw and filled an old flowerpot with pellets before going outside again.

It was still warm. Next door someone was mowing the lawn and two cats were fighting noisily somewhere nearby. Cats! No problem, Charlie thought. Isolde would soon see them off.

She was just laying a trail of chicken feed from the gate to the henhouse when she heard the phone ring. She ran into the house. 'Hello?' she said breathlessly.

'Where did you just come from?' her gran hissed into her ear. 'The phone rang at least ten times.'

'Me? Why? I was in the garden,' stuttered Charlie. Her heart was beating so loud that she thought her grandma must be able to hear it.

'Is something wrong?'

'Why? No. Everything's fine.' Charlie's gran usually knew when Charlie was lying, because she always blushed. 'As red as cherry jam,' Grandma Slater would say. But luckily she couldn't see Charlie's face down the phone.

'Hmm. You'd better be keeping that henhouse latched. You know how easily the door swings open,' she said.

'Of course, Grandma!' *If she only knew*, Charlie thought, *she'd bite my head off!*

'You sound strange,' barked Grandma Slater. 'Are you ill?'

'No,' replied Charlie. 'I'm fine. Really.'

'All right, then.' Grandma Slater cleared her throat. 'And what are you still doing there anyway? Shouldn't you be home by now?'

'Mum's still working,' muttered Charlie.

'What did you say? Stop mumbling like that!'

'Mum – is – still – working,' repeated Charlie.

'Your mother works too much.'

'What else is she supposed to do?' retorted Charlie. She stuck her tongue out at the phone.

'Well, goodbye then,' grunted Grandma Slater, and put the phone down. That was how she always ended her phone calls, just plonking down the receiver. *If I ever did that . . .* Charlie thought. Then she grabbed her school bag and sat down at the kitchen table to do her homework, even though she was shaking with rage. And sick from worrying about Isolde.

Charlie woke up to the sound of the tins rattling outside. Startled, she shot to her feet – and realised she was still sitting at the kitchen table. It was pitch black outside.

Oh no, I fell asleep! she thought. Her heart was beating wildly, right up in her throat. Who could that be out there? Surely, the Piranhas must all be in their beds by now. Holding her breath, Charlie crept down the dark corridor towards the front door. What if this was a real burglar? Or someone who was looking for Grandma Slater's treasure? Charlie carefully opened the door and peered outside.

There wasn't much to be seen in the darkness, of course. But she could hear someone cursing. And that someone was coming towards the house! Charlie's hand closed around the door handle. *Got to get back to the kitchen,* she thought. *To the phone.* But she was frozen with fear.

'Charlie? For heaven's sake, switch on the light! What's all that nonsense with the tins? Do you want me to break my neck?'

'Mum?' said Charlie, dumbfounded. 'How . . . ?

Where did you come from?'

'I nearly fell asleep behind the wheel,' replied her mum. Her tired face appeared out of the darkness. 'And so I thought I'd go home early and surprise my daughter. And when I got there, what did I find?' She sighed as she leant against the doorframe. 'A note. "Mum, I'm sleeping over at Gran's." That's it. You know full well that I would never have allowed it – it's far too lonely out here.'

'Sorry!' mumbled Charlie. 'I just wasn't in the mood to stay in the empty flat.'

'It's all right.' Her mother pulled her closer. 'But please don't do it again, OK? Promise?'

Charlie nodded.

Her mother kissed her on the head and then they went into the kitchen.

'You weren't even in bed,' observed Charlie's mum. 'And how are you planning on getting through the school day tomorrow? Hmm?' She rubbed her knee in pain.

'What's wrong?' Charlie asked with concern.

'I knocked it, thanks to your little alarm system out there. That's what it's supposed to be, right? I nearly died of shock!'

'That was meant for the Piranhas.' Charlie gathered up her school things. 'Shall I make you a cup of tea?'

'Yes, please!' Her mother yawned. 'What piranhas?'

'Oh, that's Freddie's gang,' explained Charlie. 'I had a meeting here with my gang today, and the boys spied on us – and then they let the hens out.'

'Oh no, Gran's hens?' Charlie's mum dropped wearily on to the kitchen bench and put her feet up on a chair. 'I hope they're all accounted for.'

'No, they're not,' Charlie sighed. She sniffed at the various tea tins. 'It's awful. Isolde is gone!' Charlie's eyes immediately filled up. She quickly wiped them dry with her sleeve. 'Do you want rose petal or coconut tea?'

The only luxury Grandma Slater ever allowed herself was her collection of exotic teas.

'Rose petal,' said her mum. 'There'll be trouble when Gran gets back. What are we going to do?'

'Maybe Isolde will find her way back tonight,' replied Charlie. 'She's much smarter than the other hens.' But she didn't sound very confident. She carefully poured boiling water over the tea. The whole kitchen immediately smelt of roses.

'You know what?' said her mum, suddenly. 'We'll have some tea and then we'll go out and find Isolde. I have a torch.'

'That would be great!' sniffed Charlie. The tears were coming back again. 'I'm really worried.'

It was the dead of night. Grandma Slater's street only had a couple of streetlights, and the beam of Charlie's mum's torch zigzagged through the darkness like a thin white finger.

'Isolde is the white one, right?' asked her mum, quietly.

'Uh-huh.' Charlie nodded.

'That should make it easier.'

Unless she's been eaten, or run over by a car, Charlie thought.

They swept their torch over the meadows, underneath the hedgerows, and into the gardens. They stirred up two cats and one fat hedgehog, but there was no sign of a white hen. When they reached the end of the street, Charlie's mum stopped. She shook her head as she pointed the beam into the woods that stretched away for miles.

'If Isolde went in there we'll never find her,' she said. 'And, to be honest, I really don't want to go traipsing through the trees at this time of night. I'm sorry.'

Charlie looked at her unhappily.

'But what are we going to do?' she asked.

'Come on,' said her mother. She put her arm around Charlie's shoulders and together they started walking back towards the house. 'We'll think of something, I promise.'

But Charlie kept looking around her.

'We'll talk to Grandma together,' said her mother. 'And the best thing is simply to tell her the truth: that it wasn't your fault, that the boys wanted to play a joke and . . .'

'We can't do that!' cried Charlie. 'That means Gran will find out I brought the others here. She's forbidden that!' There was no holding back now. Charlie started sobbing.

Confused, her mother squeezed her closer. 'She forbade it?' she asked quietly.

Charlie nodded. She wiped her sleeve awkwardly over her face.

Charlie's mother hugged her daughter without another word.

'The boys will pay for this!' sobbed Charlie. 'Cross my heart and hope to die.'

'Get them to buy you a new hen,' suggested her mother. 'As white as Isolde. Maybe Gran won't notice.'

'Hmm.' That was far too lenient a punishment in Charlie's eyes. And anyway, Grandma Slater would definitely notice the switch. Charlie felt completely drained as she pushed open the gate. They had already put away the alarm system.

'Charlie, look!' whispered her mother. 'Over there, in the cabbage patch.'

There was something white between the cabbage heads.

'You'd better stay here,' Charlie whispered back, excited. 'I'll handle this.'

Crouching low and walking very slowly, Charlie approached the white spot in the darkness. 'Hey, Isolde?' she whispered. 'Hey, my sweet, beautiful Isolde?'

The hen clucked and stretched her neck anxiously. But when Charlie knelt in front of her on the cool ground, she squatted down and clucked contentedly.

Very carefully, Charlie pushed a hand underneath the hen's warm belly. Then she placed her other hand on top of her wings and gently lifted the hen up from the ground.

'Oh, Isolde!' she said, pressing her face into the soft feathers. She carried her favourite chicken back into the henhouse and put her between the others on the perch.

'Well,' said her mother, as Charlie came out of the henhouse again, 'now we can go home and relax, right?'

'Right. I'll just lock up.' Charlie skipped back to the house. 'Oh, Mum,' she remembered to ask as she reached the door, 'do you know what the black key on Gran's key ring is for?'

'What black key?' yawned her mother.

'Never mind,' said Charlie. 'It's not important.'

And they drove home.

'**S**o? How was it, chasing chickens?' Tom yelled at Charlie when she went into the classroom the next morning. Tom was the smallest and the loudest member of the Piranhas, and in Charlie's opinion he was absolutely useless at everything. He was always cracking jokes that only he got.

The other Piranhas were already there too: Freddie was swinging on the back of his chair, smirking and tugging at his big jug-ears, his Piranha earring hanging from his left ear. Next to Freddie sat Big Olly, chuckling stupidly. He was fiddling with a grubby deck of cards, as usual. Olly fancied himself as something of a magician and he was constantly practising some boring card trick. Standing behind Freddie and Olly, tall and broad-shouldered, was the fourth gang member: Will, also known as the Choker. His preferred method of ending an argument was the headlock. As usual, Will was doing his best Frankenstein impression.

Without a word, Charlie walked past the boys and sat down on her chair.

'We've already had to listen to them,' moaned Xa. 'It's been unbearable. Izzie is the only one they haven't made fun of.'

'Well, of course,' growled Charlie. All the boys adored Izzie. Pretty Izzie. Wonderful Izzie. She was sitting on the windowsill with Hannah, not quite so pretty now her face had gone all blotchy-red, like it always did when she got angry.

'We can't let them get away with it,' hissed Izzie. She glared icily at the grinning boys. Tom blew her a kiss. Red with rage, Izzie threw Xa's rubber at him.

The door opened and Mr Moldman, the pot-bellied biology teacher, rolled into the classroom.

'Next break, let's meet in the loo,' whispered Charlie before they all took their seats. Freddie started clucking again, and Mr Moldman took the opportunity to test him on different species of poultry. After that, the lesson progressed in relative peace.

At the first bell, all the C.H.I.X. jumped to their feet and made their way to the girls' toilets.

'Hey, off for another chat in the bog?' Tom shouted

after them. Olly added in his squeaky voice: 'Why don't you meet in the boys' for a change?' Even Will the Choker grinned at that.

'No way, they stink too much!' Charlie shouted back. 'They'll be choking on their stupid jokes soon,' she whispered to the others.

'Why? Do you have another idea?' asked Xa, looking over her shoulder.

The Piranhas were following them at a safe distance, waggling their backsides and clucking like chickens.

'Not yet,' answered Charlie. 'But we'll think of something.'

They had reached the girls' loo. 'I think they're following us,' whispered Hannah, anxiously.

'They won't dare come in here,' said Charlie.

And although the Piranhas clucked, crowed and flapped their wings, they stayed outside.

'Xa, you climb on the lid and keep a look out,' ordered Charlie, as they all crammed into the tiny cubicle.

'I thought you said they wouldn't dare come in here?' said Izzie.

Charlie shrugged. 'You never know with that bunch of idiots.'

'Did you find your hen?' asked Hannah.

Charlie nodded and rubbed her nose. 'Yes, luckily. But just think how scared the poor thing must have been. The Piranhas will have to pay.'

'Yes, and for their stupid comments, too,' chimed in Izzie. She felt her cheeks, where two red blotches still remained.

'Well, we do have one advantage,' said Charlie. 'We know where the Piranhas hang out.'

Xa nodded. 'In the woods behind the scrapyard. Everybody knows that.'

'Exactly. They've built a shack there, from all sorts of rubbish.'

'No! They have a treehouse now,' said Izzie. 'It's great. It's way up high in a dead tree.'

'Really?' Charlie eyed her suspiciously. 'And how would you know about that?'

Izzie's face turned really red, all the way to the tips of her blonde hair. 'How do you think?' she retorted. 'I've been there. Freddie invited me.'

Charlie whistled, pretending to be impressed. 'Oooh, you were invited!'

'Don't be an idiot,' hissed Izzie. 'The boys aren't always as bad as you think.'

'No? So what about yesterday, then?' Charlie hit back. 'Was that "not as bad as we thought"?'

'Shhh,' whispered Xa suddenly from above. 'Tom's in here.'

'What?' Charlie squeezed past Izzie and the dumb-founded Hannah and tore open the cubicle door.

There was Tom, giggling and wiggling his hips. He had scraped his hair into a tiny Mohican sticking up from his head.

'Coo-ee!' he squawked. 'Have we already finished our really secret meeting? Such a shame!'

Two younger girls, who had just come in, giggled madly. But an older girl, who was fixing her hair in front of the mirror, grabbed Tom by the collar and shoved him through the door without a word.

'Thank you,' Xa called down from her lookout.

'Don't mention it,' the older girl replied. And she went back to her hair.

Charlie, Izzie and Hannah squeezed back into the cubicle.

'So they have a treehouse,' Charlie said. 'That makes things much easier.'

Hannah looked at her in surprise. 'Why? I don't understand.'

'Just think for a second,' Charlie said.

'I know,' Xa blurted out. She jumped down from the lid of the toilet.

'Of course,' Izzie laughed out loud.

Only Hannah shrugged, still completely lost.

'OK,' Charlie sighed, 'I'll explain. Listen . . .'

Chapter Seven

After school, Charlie went home with Xa. Xa's mum had invited Charlie for tea, and Charlie was quite happy about that. In the past few days she'd had to cook for herself – eggs and baked potatoes. That was all she knew how to cook.

'Just don't start arguing with Titus again,' pleaded Xa, as they climbed the stairs to the fourth floor.

'I can't promise. He's such a pain sometimes.'

'He's really not that bad. You just don't like boys.'

'Exactly. They're all idiots.'

Xa sighed. 'You're already as grumpy as your gran. Is it contagious or something?'

That stung. For the next two minutes, Charlie silently chewed her lip. If anyone else had said that to her she would have immediately turned around and gone home. But Xa was her best friend, and she'd only get upset if Charlie just left her standing. Once she'd not spoken to Charlie for a week. A whole week!

'So,' Charlie just mumbled. 'You're always protecting your big brother.'

'That's not true,' said Xa. 'But he *is* my brother. It's hard for you to understand because you don't have one.'

'Thank goodness for that,' replied Charlie. 'That would be all I need.' Who would ever wish for a brother? Not her, that was for sure.

At first the meal was a peaceful affair. They had spaghetti, especially for Charlie, and Xa's dad told one joke after another until Charlie was nearly choking with laughter. Titus, Xa's older brother, was busy with his food, which kept him quiet.

But then, just as Charlie was enjoying the delicious dessert, Xa's mother said: 'I'm meeting the girls for a coffee later. Maybe Charlie would like to keep you company and the two of you can look after Luke? OK?'

Xa's spoon stopped in mid-air. Charlie forgot to swallow.

'But we're doing something *very* important this afternoon,' said Xa.

'What's that?' asked her father. 'Something for school?'

Charlie and Xa shook their heads.

'Well, then, you can postpone it until tomorrow, right?'

'Can't Titus look after him for a change?'

'I have football,' Titus interrupted through a mouthful of food.

'Xa, really,' said her mother.

Xa stared in silence at her plate.

Charlie kicked her under the table, but Xa still didn't say anything.

Titus kept chomping away, as if the whole thing had nothing to do with him. Charlie could have exploded with rage. She gave Xa's mum a pleading look.

'This really is important,' Charlie said. 'Xa has to be there. She really has to.'

Xa's mum gave an awkward laugh. 'And what is it that's so important? Go on, out with it, Xa.'

Xa shook her head. 'I can't. It's a secret.'

'Ha! Will you listen to that,' Titus smirked and shook his head.

'That's enough,' said Xa's father. 'Let's eat in peace. We can't please all our children all of the time.'

'Titus is a boy and that's the only reason he doesn't have to look after Luke,' muttered Charlie under her breath. 'Just because he's a stupid *boy*.'

Xa's parents looked at her in surprise. Xa still didn't say anything. But her face had turned white.

'But that's nonsense, Charlotte,' said Xa's mother.

'And it's none of your business anyway,' growled Titus across the table.

'Oh, just shut up!' hissed Charlie.

'That's enough,' interjected Xa's father, angrily. 'Next time it'll be Titus's turn to look after Luke, but today it's Xa's job. And now I don't want to hear another word!'

'Agreed?' Xa's mother took her daughter's hand.

Xa looked at her mum, and nodded.

Titus gave Charlie a broad grin. Then he took another helping of spaghetti.

That was too much for Charlie. Without another word, she got up, ran into the hall, grabbed her bag and ran out the front door. It slammed behind her.

The C.H.I.X. had agreed to meet at the scrapyard. By the time Charlie arrived, out of breath, Izzie and Hannah were already waiting. Hannah was eating a chocolate bar.

'Where's Xa?' asked Izzie, surprised. 'Weren't you two supposed to come together?'

'Xa has to babysit,' scowled Charlie.

'Well, I'm glad I don't have a little brother,' sighed Izzie.

'Oh, I would love to,' said Hannah. 'But my parents don't want one.'

'We'd better leave our bikes here,' said Charlie. She nudged Izzie. 'You go in front. You know the way.'

The small wood where the Piranhas had their den started right behind the fence that surrounded the scrapyard. There were a few footpaths, but the C.H.I.X. didn't use those, of course. For once Izzie was not wearing a dress, but a pair of leggings, and she led the way, without hesitating, through the undergrowth and deeper into the wood. Soon the scrapyard had disappeared behind them and they were surrounded by nothing but tall trees and ferns.

'It's over there,' whispered Izzie. In front of them was a brackish pond covered with green algae. Near the shore stood a tall old tree. The trunk grew out of the water and its crown was bare, and in it the Piranhas had built their treehouse. It was made from old planks of wood that had been painted in every colour imaginable. For a roof the boys had just used an old sunshade. The floor was covered with carpets from the scrapyard. Leading up to the 'house' was a rickety home-made ladder.

'Wow!' whispered Charlie.

The Piranhas were at home. They were sitting on the platform, their legs dangling over the edge, and they were eating crisps.

A radio was blaring all the way down to where the C.H.I.X. were hiding.

'Handy,' whispered Izzie. 'They couldn't hear us over that racket if we rode up on an elephant.'

'Yeah,' chuckled Hannah.

'Yes, but they could still see us,' Charlie whispered back.

'Too right. You get a great view from up there,' breathed Izzie.

'And you would know about that, of course,' muttered Charlie. Izzie made a face at her.

Charlie rubbed her nose. That usually helped her think. But there really wasn't much to think about.

'We'll just have to risk it,' she whispered. 'Those bushes grow nearly all the way to the ladder. And then it's just a matter of speed. Ready?'

The other two nodded.

'Let's go then,' whispered Charlie. They crept silently towards the treehouse, although with all the noise from the radio it wasn't really necessary.

The Piranhas' feet were still dangling happily above the girls' heads.

'This is for Isolde,' breathed Charlie.

They ran out from the bushes and over the slippery ground to the ladder – and pushed it over. The ladder swayed through the air as if in slow motion, until it finally tipped over and dropped with a loud splash into the pond.

By the time the stunned faces of Tom, Freddie, Olly

and Will appeared at the edge of the platform, it was all over.

The C.H.I.X. performed a victory dance.

'Whoohoooo,' they screamed. 'Yeeee-haa!' Green pond scum ran down their arms where the ladder had splattered them.

'Hey!' yelled Freddie. Will switched off the radio.

'Are you crazy?' Tom's voice nearly cracked with fury. 'Put that ladder back!'

But that just encouraged another squeal of laughter from the C.H.I.X.

'Cowards! Let this be a lesson to you,' Charlie shouted up at them, while Izzie and Hannah were still doubled over with the giggles. 'Next time you want to pick a fight, come straight to us and don't take it out on some innocent hens.'

'But that was just a joke!' Big Olly shouted back.

'Well, this is just a joke too,' replied Charlie. 'Goodbye, and enjoy the view.'

'What do you mean?' yelled Freddie. In his rage, he nearly fell out of the tree. 'You can't just leave us here!'

'Of course we can,' Izzie shouted back. 'Yesterday you left us to catch the hens.'

'Put that ladder back right now,' howled Will. 'Or there will be trouble.' His face was crimson.

'Like what?' Charlie asked. Hannah nearly choked with laughter.

'Come on,' Charlie linked arms with Izzie and Hannah. 'We're off. Oh . . .' and she turned around once more, 'I don't quite understand how you can have been stupid enough not to fasten your ladder to the tree.'

'Stay there!' yelled Tom.

'Come back,' pleaded Freddie.

'We'll get you for this!' howled Olly.

But the C.H.I.X. had already vanished back into the undergrowth.

Chapter Eight

An hour later Charlie, Izzie and Hannah were sitting next to each other on Grandma Slater's sofa, still giggling.

'Hey, come back!' Charlie mimicked Freddie, and the others nearly slid under the table with laughter.

'Tom was leaping around like a mad chimp,' snorted Izzie.

'Please, stop,' groaned Hannah, wiping tears from her eyes. 'I'm already aching all over.'

'Did you see the Choker?' Charlie tilted her head and rolled her eyes like Will when he was angry. 'He's getting seriously like Frankenstein.'

'Stop!' panted Hannah. 'Stop it, or I'll explode.'

Charlie jumped to her feet. 'You know what? We deserve a reward.' She fetched Grandma Slater's forbidden biscuits from the cupboard and put the large tin on the table. So what if Gran told her off and didn't speak to her for three days? It didn't matter. Today nothing mattered.

Delighted, Hannah took a chocolate cookie.

Izzie twirled her biscuit like a champagne glass. 'To the greatest gang in the world,' she called. 'Cheers!'

Giggling, all three of them stuffed themselves with the forbidden treats.

'To the C.H.I.X.!' exclaimed Hannah, reaching for another biscuit.

'You know what?' said Izzie. 'Now we can solve the mystery of the black key.'

'Exactly.' Charlie took the key ring from her pocket. Izzie and Hannah eyed it expertly.

'Well, it wouldn't fit into a strongbox or safe or anything like that,' declared Izzie. 'It's too big. Looks more like a cellar key.'

'My gran doesn't have a cellar,' Charlie said. 'There's only the store cupboard and the attic.'

'The attic sounds good,' said Izzie. 'Most people hide their secrets in the attic. At least, that's how it is in the movies.'

Charlie rubbed her nose. 'Gran says her attic is haunted.'

'Nonsense,' Izzie got up. 'She only says that to stop you from snooping around up there.'

'Probably,' Charlie mumbled.

Grinning, Izzie pulled Hannah up from the sofa. 'Definitely. Or do you believe in ghosts? Your gran's quite crafty.'

And so Charlie led Izzie and Hannah up the stairs to where her gran's bedroom was, as well as the tiny box-room where Charlie sometimes slept.

'Is that your mum?' Izzie stopped in front of one of the many yellowing photographs that hung in tarnished silver frames all over the walls.

Charlie nodded. 'That's when she was eighteen or so.'

'And that one, up there?' Hannah stood on her toes. 'Is that her as a child?'

'Mmm,' said Charlie, opening the attic hatch above their heads and pulling down the ladder. She frowned up at the black hole in the ceiling. Izzie and Hannah were still standing in front of the photographs.

'You don't really look like your mum at all,' observed Izzie. 'Do you get your blonde hair from your dad?'

'No idea,' muttered Charlie. 'Are you coming or what?'

'Oh, sorry, you don't really know your father, do you?' said Izzie. She pushed past Charlie and climbed up the ladder. Charlie pressed her lips together. First the thing about the ghosts, and now this reminder. Her good mood had evaporated.

'Don't you even know what he looks like?' asked Hannah inquisitively.

'No! And I don't care, either,' replied Charlie. 'Could we change the subject, please?' She climbed quickly after Izzie. She'd much rather deal with ghosts that might or might not exist than with a load of stupid questions.

'No dad,' mumbled Hannah behind her. 'Wouldn't that be great?'

Charlie looked around in surprise. Shyly, Hannah returned her glance.

'Hey, this is a great attic,' Izzie shouted from above. 'Where are you guys?'

'Coming,' Charlie called back. She scaled the last few rungs of the ladder.

'Isn't this fab?' said Izzie. 'Just look at all the stuff up here.'

'Fab,' agreed Hannah.

Charlie said nothing. She looked around uneasily, but at least there was no sign of ghosts or anything like that. 'Yep, my gran likes to keep everything,' she said, finally. 'It's annoying, but sometimes it's a good thing.'

'I think attics are really exciting.' Eyes gleaming, Izzie started rummaging through Grandma Slater's boxes and crates. Hannah followed her lead but Charlie just stood by the hatch and felt uncomfortable. She tried hard to feel how she had felt in the kitchen. But it didn't work. Forbidden biscuits were one thing; this was different. What if her gran discovered that she had been up here? She knew Charlie would never dare to come up by herself. She watched as Hannah and Izzie touched, lifted and opened everything.

'Hey, aren't we looking for a lock or something?' she said, waving the black key at them.

'Yes, yes.' Izzie was staring with delight into a huge box. 'Ooh! Look at this, lots of old dresses. With lace and stuff.' She giggled as she put on a tiny hat. 'What do I look like?'

'There's a mirror over there,' mumbled Charlie. 'Go and look yourself.'

'What's the matter?' asked Izzie. 'What's made you all cross?'

'Over here,' Hannah called out excitedly. 'There's a lock on this trunk and it looks just right.'

Izzie and Charlie picked their way towards her.

'This is so exciting,' whispered Izzie.

Charlie tried the black key in the lock. It did go in, but it wouldn't turn. 'Doesn't fit,' she said, disappointed.

'It doesn't matter,' said Izzie. She looked around. 'There are plenty more places to try up here. Look over there, in the corner. That chest with the shoes on it.'

'It's got three key holes,' observed Hannah, sneezing. The dust they had stirred up tickled their noses terribly.

The three girls climbed over old toys and rolled-up carpets until they stood in front of the chest. It had huge drawers, each one with a key hole.

'Go on, Charlie,' Izzie was fizzing with excitement. Hannah was chewing her thumbnail in anticipation.

Charlie put the black key into the topmost lock. She shook her head.

'Doesn't fit either, but . . .' Charlie pulled on the handle, '. . . it's open anyway.'

The three C.H.I.X. peered into the drawer.

In it, neatly folded, were romper suits, bibs, tiny shirts and baby shoes.

'Oh, Charlie!' chuckled Izzie. 'These must be yours!'

'How cute!' said Hannah with delight.

Charlie blushed.

'Next one!' she said, quickly pushing the drawer shut. She put the key into the second lock. 'Nope!'

But the second drawer was also unlocked, and it contained more of Charlie's outgrown clothes – although larger than those in the previous drawer. Lots of hand-knitted jumpers, scarves and gloves, with mothballs sprinkled among them.

'My gran's always knitting things for me too,' said Hannah. 'They're horribly scratchy.'

'My gran's things don't scratch.' Charlie sighed as she pushed the drawer shut. 'But they're always too small. Or the sleeves are far too long. I always look like a sausage in them. But there's trouble if I don't wear them. You should hear my gran going on about how ungrateful I am. "Just like your mother, blah, blah, blah".'

'Don't your mum and your gran get along?' asked Izzie.

Charlie shrugged. 'They don't really fight, but they're never very nice to each other.'

The key didn't fit in the third lock either. Anyway, Charlie wasn't in the mood to look any more.

'Both my grannies are lovely,' said Hannah. 'Especially one of them. She's heaven-sent, my father always says.'

'My mum and my gran,' Izzie brushed some cobwebs from her hair, 'are always arguing. It's quite scary. And my gran actually lives with us. I can tell you . . .'

But Hannah had pulled the third drawer open and was looking inside. 'Wow! Loads of soppy novels. My grannies read this stuff as well.'

Charlie looked at the piles of thin paperbacks in surprise. They had wonderful titles, like *Heart Beat*, or *Love Till The End*.

'I didn't know my gran read such things,' mumbled Charlie. She leafed through one of the books. Suddenly she began to giggle. 'It would be great to tease her about these.'

'Yes, but then she'd know that you'd been snooping around up here,' said Izzie.

'You're right.' Charlie sighed. She suddenly felt bad again. But she tried not to show it, and the three of them continued their search a little longer.

They found crates full of old china, boxes full of books, and lots of mended clothes. They found a broken sewing machine, a dusty butterfly collection, mouldy stamp albums and a box containing a wig. But there was no sign of a lock that the black key might fit. Finally Hannah looked at her watch. 'Oh no, it's gone six already. I have to get home.'

'After six?' Izzie exclaimed. 'I was supposed to go to the shops.'

'We can always carry on tomorrow,' said Charlie. 'I don't think we'll find anything up here anyway.' She had had enough of going through Grandma Slater's old things, but she couldn't say that, of course.

They climbed down the ladder.

'What were you supposed to buy at the shops?'

'Eggs, potatoes and stuff. Why?'

'No problem.' Charlie latched the ladder back in place. 'I have all that here.'

Baffled, Izzie looked at her. 'Oh, of course. I never thought of that.'

Charlie laughed, embarrassed. 'I'll just quickly lock up the house and then we'll grab some things for you.

I'm going home as well. My mum's coming back early today.'

When they stepped outside the sky had clouded over, but the air was still mild and the evening tasted of summer.

Izzie ran over to her bike and fetched her shopping bag.

'Here, it says . . .' she frowned at her shopping list, '. . . ten eggs, a kilo of potatoes, runner beans, parsley.'

Charlie nodded. 'Not a problem.' She took the bag from Izzie and ran off to the vegetable patch. 'Let's start with the beans,' she said. 'Did you know they're meant to be poisonous if you eat them raw?'

Izzie and Hannah shook their heads.

With quick fingers, Charlie picked a little heap of long, slender pods from their beanpoles. 'These here are the best,' she said. 'Very tender, and not stringy at all.'

Izzie just mumbled: 'Oh!'

'How much parsley do you need?'

Izzie shrugged helplessly.

Charlie plucked two large handfuls that grew among the beans. 'Smell this!' she said proudly, holding a bunch under their noses. 'My gran always sows the annual variety. It's much stronger.'

Hannah and Izzie looked at each other.

'How do you know all this?' asked Hannah.

'Oh, you just kind of pick it up.' Charlie rubbed her nose. She got to her feet and went over to the next vegetable bed, which was quite a bit wider than the bean patch.

'I can't give you that many potatoes,' she said, plunging her hands into the dark earth. 'My gran's pretty stingy when it comes to those. But they'll still taste much better than the ones from the shops.'

'Oh, this is great,' said Izzie. 'My bag's already quite full. I just need some eggs.'

'Coming up.' Charlie jumped to her feet and together they ran to the henhouse. The hens, of course, were asleep again. Charlie already had half an eggbox full in the storeroom. She quickly filled it up.

'My mum's going to love this,' said Izzie as they ran back to their bikes.

Hannah suddenly giggled. 'I wonder how the Piranhas are doing.'

Charlie cast an expert glance at the sky. 'Well, as long as it's not raining . . .'

'You really think they're still up there?' Hannah sounded a little concerned.

'No. They've probably been rescued by someone walking their dog in the wood,' said Charlie. 'And if not, we'll know tomorrow, when school starts. Oh, by the way,' Charlie grinned, 'tomorrow you can give me a hand mucking out the henhouse.'

'Oh yes, please!' said Hannah, excitedly.

'Mucking out?' Izzie pulled a face. 'What do you wear for that?'

'Your best dress, of course,' replied Charlie. For the longest moment she and Izzie just looked at each other, then they both grinned.

'See you tomorrow,' Charlie swung herself on to her bike.

'See you tomorrow,' Hannah called after her. 'I hope Xa can come this time.'

'Hope so,' Charlie called back. But the mention of Xa had managed to spoil her mood.

Chapter
Nine

When Charlie got home, she had a visitor waiting for her.

'Your best friend is here,' said her mother.

'Xa?' asked Charlie.

'Of course Xa.' Her mother looked at her in surprise. 'Or do you have another best friend?'

Charlie shook her head and rubbed her nose hard.

'Did you fall out?'

'Not really.'

'Ah. I'd better not ask any more questions, is that it?' Her mother shook her head. 'Shall I make you some sandwiches?'

'Yes, please.' Charlie walked slowly towards her room. She still wanted to be angry with Xa, but she was just relieved that she had come round. Xa could ignore her for days when she was sulking. Even at school, where they sat next to each other in class! She really could be stubborn.

But what does Xa have to sulk about? Charlie put her hand on the door handle. *If anybody should be sulking, it's me,* she thought. Her head and her heart were in a right muddle.

Xa was sitting on Charlie's bed. Her eyes were red and she looked a little lost. She gave Charlie a small smile.

'Hello,' she said. 'How did it go? Did our plan work?'

Charlie nodded. 'You missed out.' She sat down at her desk and stared at the carpet. 'Izzie and Hannah were great.'

'Really?' asked Xa, quietly. Then the two of them sat in silence for what seemed ages. Xa nibbled on her fingernails and Charlie rubbed her nose. Luckily, Charlie's mum came in with the sandwiches.

'What do you want to drink?' she asked. 'Hot chocolate?'

'Yes, please,' said Xa. She managed a wobbly smile.

Charlie just nodded.

Her mother went out and they were left in silence again.

Charlie took a salami sandwich, then put it back on the plate.

'What did you tell the others?' asked Xa.

'That you had to babysit. What else?'

Xa fiddled with her ear. The chicken feather hung from a leather band around her neck.

'Thanks for trying to help me,' said Xa in a tiny voice. She still didn't look at Charlie.

'So why didn't you say anything?' Charlie burst out. 'I felt like such an idiot. Did you see your stupid brother grinning at me? And you just sat there as if it was nothing to do with you. But I was right. I was completely right!'

Xa looked at her hands. 'I can't do that,' she said, so quietly that Charlie could hardly hear her.

'Can't do what?' Charlie shook her head in frustration.

'If my mum asks me something, I can't say no. And when my dad joins in, well . . .' Xa shrugged.

'Hmm.' Charlie grabbed the sandwich again. 'Your brother . . .' she said, her words muffled by her mouthful, '. . . is really good at saying no.'

'I know he is,' mumbled Xa. She nibbled at a cheese sandwich and sniffed.

'Are you crying?' asked Charlie, startled.

'I'm fine, really,' answered Xa. She blew her nose. And by the time Charlie's mum came and interrupted with the hot chocolate, both girls were happy again.

'Here we go,' she said, putting two steaming mugs on the table. 'I hope there's enough sugar in there. Do you need anything else?'

Charlie shook her head.

'I have to go soon anyway,' said Xa. When they were alone again, she said to Charlie: 'You don't always fight back either.'

'What do you mean?' Charlie frowned, though she knew exactly what Xa was talking about.

'Well, with your gran. Do you ever say no to her?'

'That's different,' cried Charlie. 'Nobody says no to my gran. Not even my mum. And if she does, Gran doesn't speak to us for a fortnight and won't let me stay with her until my mum has apologised. Are your parents like that?'

'No, but . . .'

'No, they're not a bit like that! And you should be really, really happy about it.' Charlie stopped talking. Her heart was beating wildly and her bottom lip was trembling. She quickly grabbed another sandwich and bit into it.

Xa looked at her, confused. 'How was I to know it's that bad? You never told me.'

'Well, it *is* that bad,' said Charlie. 'And I don't want to talk about it any more. There's nothing I can do about it anyway.'

'Maybe you could come to us more often when your mum's working?' suggested Xa.

'No, but thank you. I'd just fight with your brother all the time,' said Charlie, though the thought did make her smile. 'Anyway, while you were babysitting, and we were safe from the Piranhas, we searched the whole attic for the lock for the black key.'

'And?'

'Nothing. And I've tried all the locks in the rooms downstairs. It's a real mystery. Do you know what I think?'

'What?' Xa slurped her hot chocolate. It made her feel lovely and warm.

'I think Grandma Slater just wanted to play a trick on me,' whispered Charlie. 'I wouldn't put it past her.'

'Then there's no point looking for the lock,' said Xa.

'Oh yes, there is!' Charlie frowned. 'We should definitely keep looking. Just in case. Wouldn't it be great if we really found treasure? Those stupid Piranhas would probably explode with envy.'

'Are we doing anything tomorrow?' asked Xa. Then she added, 'I don't have to babysit Luke all week. Mum says it's Titus's turn.'

'What? Now you tell me!' said Charlie. 'So the whole fight was worth it. We're mucking out the hen-house tomorrow. Will you come?'

Xa nodded as she got up. 'Do you think the boys are still in their treehouse?'

'No, definitely not,' answered Charlie. And she was right. The Piranhas had been home for half an hour. And they were furious.

Chapter Ten

Revenge is a strange thing. There never seems to be an end to it.

As Charlie wheeled her bicycle into the playground the next morning, the Piranhas jumped out of the bushes at her. Tom and Olly pulled her from her bike and Will grabbed her in his well-known chokehold.

'Hey!' gasped Charlie, once she was over the initial shock. 'Are you crazy? We'll all be late!'

'*We'll* be in class in a few minutes,' replied Freddie, with a smirk. '*You*, however, are taking the day off.'

They dragged Charlie, kicking and screaming, behind the school building. The bell had gone for the first lesson and the playground was completely deserted.

Charlie soon realised that they were headed for the

small shed where Mr Mower the caretaker kept his brooms, rakes and shovels.

'Open it!' ordered Freddie with a smug grin on his face. To Charlie's great surprise, Olly produced a key from his pocket.

'Where did you get that?' she asked. 'You stole it from Mower!'

'No, we just borrowed it!' replied Olly, in mock indignation. 'It's his spare.'

'So that's what you've been practising your magic tricks for – training your fingers to nick things,' snorted Charlie. But at that moment Will the Choker shoved her into the windowless, dark shed.

'Oh no,' Izzie's voice came out of the gloom. 'We were hoping at least *you'd* get away. This is so embarrassing.'

'They just grabbed us and nobody came to help.' Hannah sounded upset.

'Well, there's no point moaning about it.' Charlie carefully edged forwards, but she stepped on a rake and the handle whacked her on the head. 'Ouch!'

'What is it?' asked Xa, concerned.

'Nothing. Does anyone have a torch?'

'Nope,' answered Izzie.

'What a well-prepared gang we are,' moaned Charlie. She felt her head. There was going to be a huge bump.

'But they can't just leave us locked up in here,' snivelled Hannah. 'School starts soon.'

'It already has,' observed Izzie. 'And it won't be them who'll be in trouble. Or do you think Mrs Rose is going to believe our story?'

'But she has to,' Hannah whined. 'I was late twice last week. If my dad finds out . . .'

'Calm down,' said Charlie. 'When someone finds us, we'll have a witness who can say that we were definitely locked in here, right?'

'*If* someone finds us,' added Xa, gloomily, 'before we end up as skeletons against the wall.'

Hannah groaned.

'Maybe Mr Mower will come by soon,' said Charlie.

'And maybe he won't,' replied Izzie. 'How about we make some noise?'

'It's a waste of energy,' said Charlie. 'There wasn't anyone around when they dragged me in here.'

'Mrs Rose doesn't like us being late at all,' sighed Xa. 'And I'm already in her bad books. Those boys are so mean.'

The others were silent.

'After we get out of here,' growled Charlie, 'they're going to wish they'd never been born.'

'How long does it take to starve to death?' asked Hannah.

'We'd die of thirst first,' said Xa.

'Or suffocate,' muttered Charlie. 'The air in here is horrible.'

'You know what?' said Izzie. 'This whole revenge thing is really getting on my nerves. It's just going to go on and on. Next, *we'll* have to get back at them, and then they'll have to get back at *us*, and so on for ever. It's kind of boring.'

'They started it,' said Charlie.

Then from outside came the sound of footsteps and *Yankee Doodle*. Mr Mower always whistled that tune.

The C.H.I.X. started pounding on the walls of the shed.

'Let us out!' they screamed. 'Open up, Mr Mower, please!'

The door opened and the girls squinted in the light. Mr Mower stood in the doorway, baffled.

'How did you get in here?' he asked.

'We were . . .' began Hannah.

'We don't know who did it,' Charlie interrupted her quickly, 'but someone grabbed us and shoved us in here.'

'What? All of you at the same time?' said Mr Mower, in disbelief.

'Well, no, one after the other, actually,' said Charlie.

'Hmm. Right. And how did they get my key?' asked Mr Mower.

'How should we know?' said Charlie, tetchily.

'Thieves can pick locks,' suggested Xa.

'Thieves? What thieves?' Poor Mr Mower looked even more confused now.

'We have to get to class,' said Charlie, quickly pushing past the caretaker.

'Yes, and thanks for freeing us,' said Xa, before taking off after Charlie.

'Why couldn't I say who it really was?' asked Hannah, as they all ran towards the school building.

'Because that's not the way it's done between gangs,' Charlie answered impatiently.

'I don't get it!' Hannah was gasping for air.

'Izzie, you explain it to her,' sighed Charlie. She suddenly veered off towards the bike stands.

'What are you doing?' Izzie shouted after her. 'Mrs Rose will be furious already.'

Charlie didn't answer. She walked along the rows of bicycles. 'Here we are!' she said finally. 'All right next to each other. How handy.'

She quickly opened the tyre valves on four bikes. And because she wasn't quite sure if the next one was a Piranha bike too, she let the airout of that one as well, just in case.

'Oh Charlie, don't do that,' pleaded Xa.

'This is really stupid,' said Izzie. 'I'm going inside. Come on, Hannah.'

The two of them ran towards the entrance.

Xa stood next to Charlie. 'Don't you think that's enough?' she asked, hesitantly.

'Done!' said Charlie. She giggled. 'Can't wait to see their faces.'

Xa shook her head.

'Oh, stop being such a sourpuss, come on.' Charlie took her by the arm and dragged her along. 'Hey. Wait!' she shouted after Izzie and Hannah. They caught up with their friends on the front steps.

Mrs Rose listened to their story with a deep frown and pursed lips. Meanwhile, Freddie, Olly, Tom and Will sat as stiff as planks, staring at their books.

'Oh, come on,' said Mrs Rose, when Charlie had finally finished. 'How stupid do you lot think I am? First those four chumps there, suddenly so intent on their textbooks, turn up late – and then you spin me this outrageous story.'

'But it's true,' replied Charlie, meekly.

'Yes, of course it is. And I still believe in Father Christmas. Sit down!'

The C.H.I.X. skulked off to their seats. Mrs Rose picked up her little black book and made four more crosses.

'The line next to my name must look like a grave-yard by now,' Charlie muttered into Xa's ear.

'Do you want to know what I think?' said Mrs Rose,

as she dropped the book back into her shiny red bag. 'I think we are having a little gang rivalry. And since I believe gangs are probably the silliest things on this planet, I now strongly advise all of you never to be late to my class again. Have I made myself quite clear?'

The C.H.I.X. nodded.

'And you? Did you get the message as well?'

The Piranhas muttered something back.

'Fine. Then let's get your brains on your work. Freddie? To the blackboard, if you please.'

Chapter
Eleven

That afternoon Hannah was the first to arrive at Grandma Slater's house. There was no sign of the others yet. She was just opening the garden gate when she heard a rustling in the bushes behind her. She spun around – but there was nothing to be seen. A fat dachshund was trotting across the street and next door a cat was sunbathing on the rubbish bins.

She leant her bike against the hedge and ran over to the chicken run. The hens' heads bobbed up curiously when they saw her coming and they clucked feebly, as if they hadn't been fed in days.

Hannah opened the door to the henhouse to fetch some feed, then paused as she heard the rustling sound again. She couldn't tell what it was, but it sounded as if it came from the currant bushes.

'Is somebody there?' she called out.

'Of course,' Charlie said behind her, pushing open the garden gate. 'Why are you looking so worried?' Xa was with her.

'Oh, it's you,' Hannah sighed with relief. A huge blackbird came out of the berry bushes to pick at the gravel path. 'I'm seeing ghosts.'

'Happens to me all the time,' said Charlie. 'Especially when I'm alone. I sometimes think my granddad is haunting this place.'

At that moment Izzie arrived.

'I don't believe it,' Charlie exclaimed. 'Izzie in wellies!'

Izzie stuck her tongue out and leant her bike against the hedge. 'We're probably the only gang that muck out henhouses together,' she sighed.

'I think it's going to be fun,' said Hannah.

'I'd rather solve the mystery of the black key,' said Xa. 'I missed the last treasure hunt.'

'Work before play,' grinned Charlie. 'Come on.'

'And how long will I smell of chicken poo after this?' Izzie asked as she trudged after the others.

'A week? A month?' smirked Charlie.

'If it's still this hot later, maybe we can cool off under the garden hose?' suggested Xa.

'Oh yes,' cried Hannah.

Two of the hens were sheltering from the summer

heat inside the henhouse. But when the four girls turned up with their pitchforks, buckets and shovels, they soon escaped, squawking in protest.

'First all that dirty straw has to come out,' ordered Charlie. 'Just chuck it through the window on to the muck heap. Then we'll scrape the poo from the perches and put new straw underneath. Oh, and most importantly, the nesting boxes. They have to be cleaned thoroughly, and the china eggs too.'

'What china eggs?' asked Xa.

'Gran says hens prefer to lay an egg next to one that's already there, rather than in an empty nest,' explained Charlie. 'That way they also think we're not stealing all of their eggs. But you've no idea how many times I've taken those stupid china ones into the house, thinking they were the real thing.'

'I want to do the nesting boxes,' Hannah called out. 'Can I?'

'Eew! There's poo everywhere,' moaned Izzie. 'And all this from a few scrawny hens?'

Charlie laughed. 'Well, nobody has invented a toilet for chickens yet. And as my gran always says: chicken poo is worth its weight in gold.'

'How come?' Izzie's face was screwed up in disgust as she scraped at the perches with a shovel.

'What do you think makes all that veg grow so well out there? It's the best fertiliser ever. You just have to remember to mix it with straw and soil, or else it gets too hot.'

'It gets too *what?*' asked Hannah.

'Hot. Too sulphurous. Too strong,' Charlie explained. 'The vegetables would shoot up without any flavour. Oh, I hope we have enough fresh straw.'

'Too much information, more like,' said Xa, as she hauled the straw in through the window.

'What should we do with the real eggs?' asked Hannah.

'Put them in the shelter outside,' said Charlie.

'Hey, there are some more here,' called out Xa. 'Way back here, underneath the perch.'

'Oh, another secret nest!' said Charlie. 'They do that sometimes. Maybe we'll find others.'

'Well, it's not fair that they get their eggs stolen all the time,' said Izzie. She was scraping beneath the perches.

'Would they all turn into little chicks?' asked Hannah. She looked uneasily at the egg in her hand.

'Of course not,' Charlie giggled. 'How would that work without a cockerel?'

'Oh . . . right!' muttered Hannah, her face bright red.

'Don't worry,' Charlie said to her. 'The hens think they have chicks in them too. They even sit on them and try to hatch them.'

After an hour the henhouse was so clean that even Grandma Slater wouldn't have found anything to complain about. The fresh straw smelt wonderful and the girls were really quite pleased with themselves.

'And now let's hose ourselves down!' said Charlie. 'Out the back, by the water butt. Nobody can see us there.'

'Yuck! My clothes are really sweaty,' said Xa. 'Do you have anything clean I could wear?'

'I brought something to change into,' said Izzie. She ran to her bike and came back with a big plastic bag.

'I don't believe you,' said Charlie, rolling her eyes. She fetched some fresh t-shirts for Xa and Hannah. Grandma Slater's rain butt was behind the house on a small bricked patch. It was surrounded by high lilacs. The girls hung their mucky clothes on the bushes and put their clean ones on a chair, safely away from the hose. Charlie turned on the ice-cold water.

Screaming and laughing in nothing but their underwear, the girls jumped around in the cold jet of water. They squirted each other and danced on the slippery bricks until their lips were blue from the cold.

It happened just as Charlie went to turn off the water.

A pair of arms appeared through the lilacs, and pulled their clothes from the branches. More arms grabbed the clean stuff from the chair, and Izzie's plastic bag. It all happened so quickly that the girls could only stand there and gape.

'Woo-hoo.' Three boys' heads grinned at them from the bushes.

'Tsk, tsk!' Tom tutted. 'Dancing around in your knickers! That's not very proper. What if the neighbours see you like that?'

'Go away!' yelled Charlie. Xa hid behind the water butt and Izzie and Hannah stood behind Charlie.

'We're going,' said Tom. 'But we're taking your clothes with us. You'll get them back tomorrow. But you better not come to school like that.'

Olly giggled hysterically. Will was blushing and staring at his shoes. But then the lilac branches swung closed and the boys were gone – together with the girls' clothes.

'You creeps,' Izzie shouted after them. Shivering, the girls ran over to the bushes. Peering through them, they saw the thieves run off across Grandma Slater's vegetable beds, the clothes bundled up in their arms.

'Stop!' Charlie screamed. 'You complete morons.'

But the boys just waved and blew kisses. Then they disappeared through the gate.

The C.H.I.X. stood shaking with cold, looking at each other. Xa came out from behind the rain butt.

'That's what I must've heard earlier,' said Hannah. 'They were here the whole time.'

'Where? What are you talking about?' asked Charlie.

'Behind the currant bushes,' Hannah answered. 'I heard something rustling there earlier.'

'And you didn't tell us?' Charlie almost screamed with frustration.

'I thought . . . I . . .' Hannah pressed her hands to her wet face.

'Leave her alone,' Izzie hissed at Charlie. 'This is where all your stupid C.H.I.X. stuff has got us.'

'OK, OK. I didn't mean it,' muttered Charlie.

'Come on, let's go inside and find something to wear,' said Xa. 'Before we all catch pneumonia.'

Huddling together, the C.H.I.X. made a dash for the house. Of course, at that very moment, Mr Stringer, Grandma Slater's nosy neighbour, poked his head over the hedge.

'What are you looking at?' Charlie shouted at him before vanishing through the front door. She didn't even want to think about what Grandma Slater would be told when she got back.

Chapter Twelve

It was Izzie who thought of trying on the old-fashioned clothes in the attic. They had great fun putting on the weird skirts and dresses that hung down past their feet and made them feel like miniature grownups from long ago. Dressed up and sitting around the kitchen table, sipping blackberry tea and eating banned biscuits, they were almost ready to find the Piranhas' revenge quite funny. Until Charlie sat bolt upright and banged her mug down on the table.

'What is it?' asked Xa, startled.

'The key!' said Charlie. 'Oh no! They have the key.'

'Are you sure?' breathed Hannah.

'Of course. It was in my jeans.'

The girls looked at each other in shock.

'When did you first hear the rustling in the bushes, Hannah?'

'Just before you all arrived.'

Charlie groaned.

'And I was babbling about treasure hunts,' Xa said in dismay.

'Yes, you were,' said Izzie. 'And you even mentioned the black key. So, if they didn't hear about it during their last snoop, they definitely know now.'

'But that's awful,' groaned Hannah. 'What are we going to do?'

'Much more importantly: what are *they* going to do? We have to find out. Right now.' Charlie could no longer sit still. She jumped up, grim-faced, then looked down at herself in shock. 'Oh no! I'd forgotten about these stupid clothes. Never mind. Come on!'

'But where to?' Hannah called after her.

'To the treehouse, of course,' said Izzie. She hitched up her long skirt and ran after Charlie.

Xa was not quite so quick. She stepped on the hem of her dress and fell flat on the floor. She struggled back to her feet and ran after the others while Hannah stumbled out of the house last, her dress bunched up above her knees.

'No way can we ride bikes in this stuff,' cried Xa.

'Well, there isn't going to be any cycling anyway,' growled Charlie, her face flushed. She was standing next to their bikes. They all had flat tyres. 'But they're going to be *so* sorry.' Charlie strode back to the house. 'What's she doing now?' asked Izzie. Hannah and Xa just shrugged and went after her.

Charlie was on the phone. 'Fine. See you soon.' She had a wicked smile on her face as she put down the receiver. 'My mum's picking us up in her taxi in ten minutes. She'll take us to the scrapyard.'

'You want to creep around woods . . .' Xa plucked at the lace and frills dangling around her legs, '. . . in these things?'

'Do you have a better idea?' asked Charlie, crossly. 'Do you think I'm just going to sit here and wait until they turn up with the key and steal my grandma's treasure?'

Hannah opened her mouth to say something, but at that moment the phone rang. Charlie picked it up and her face turned as white as chalk.

'Oh, hi, Grandma . . . no, I just thought it might be Mum. Yes, of course, everything's fine.'

Izzie smothered a giggle. Xa screwed up her face. Charlie still looked pale.

'Today we – ehm – *I* tidied up here. The weeds? Well . . . they're growing.' Xa rolled her eyes. 'Of course, absolutely.'

A car honked outside. Izzie ran to the window and peered out.

'It's your mum!' she whispered.

'Gran? I have to go. Mum's picking us up right now. What? Did I say *us*? No, just a slip of the tongue. Of course I'm alone. I know. No strangers. Yes. Yes. Bye, then. Yes, bye.'

Charlie heaved a deep sigh as she put down the phone. To her surprise, she realised that her heart wasn't beating half as fast as it usually did after one of her gran's calls. Even though she had just lied to her.

'You know what?' Charlie said to the others. 'I wish you were always next to me when my gran calls. Makes it less horrible, somehow.'

They stepped outside and Charlie locked the door.

'Did I say *us*?' mimicked Izzie, in a high voice. 'No, just a slip of the tongue.'

Giggling, they ran towards the gate.

'Doesn't she let you have anyone over?' asked Xa.

'Not a chance,' said Charlie. 'My gran usually assumes the worst of other people. Trust no one – that's her motto.'

'Not even your friends?' asked Izzie. Charlie's mum was already waving at them.

Charlie waved back and opened the gate. 'There are no such things as friends as far as my gran is concerned. She thinks everyone wants to cheat her, or rob her, or steal her handbag.'

'Oh dear,' mumbled Xa.

'So?' Charlie's mother called to them. 'As your chauffeur, may I enquire as to your plans, and why the strange attire?'

'Sorry, Mum,' said Charlie. She dropped into the passenger seat. 'It's top secret.'

Chapter
Thirteen

'I can only see three pairs of feet,' whispered Xa.

They had sneaked up to the Piranhas' treehouse, and the owners' dirty feet were dangling above their heads. The boys had tied strings to some crooked branches and let them hang into the pond's green water. They were supposed to be fishing lines.

'Maybe they posted a lookout,' whispered Hannah. She glanced anxiously around them.

'Wait here. I'll do a quick recce,' hissed Izzie. Despite the long dress, she slunk as nimbly as a cat into the undergrowth. An empty drink can flew down from the treehouse into the water.

'Hey, Tom. Stop it!' shouted Freddie. 'You want it to look like a dump around here, or what?'

'OK, OK,' replied Tom.

'And that's enough messing about. It's time to make a plan,' said Freddie.

'Yeah, Boss,' joined in Will. 'Any ideas?'

'*Boss!*' giggled Xa.

'Looks like we came at the right time,' muttered Charlie.

The undergrowth behind them rustled and Izzie crouched down next to them in the grass. 'Olly's sitting in the bushes about twenty metres from here,' she whispered. 'But he's totally into some stupid card trick.'

At that very moment, Freddie shouted from above: 'Hey, Olly? Are you keeping watch?'

'Ye-es!' Olly squeaked from the undergrowth.

'Fine,' Freddie said. 'Then I'll tell you my plan.'

'I hope it's not one of your long ones,' groaned Will.

'No. Even you should be able to understand it,' replied Freddie. 'First, we have to make sure that those stupid girls are at home tonight.'

'Why shouldn't they be at home?' Will sounded puzzled.

'Doh! You're dense sometimes,' sighed Freddie. 'Because they know we have the key.'

'No way will they be out,' Tom sneered. 'They're going to be crying on their mummies' shoulders tonight. After they get home in their knickers.'

The Piranhas kicked their legs with glee. Down below, the C.H.I.X. were boiling with rage.

'OK, boys, seriously,' said Freddie, in his best commando voice. 'I'll check if Charlie's going to be at home.'

'You'd better hope her mum's not working,' said Tom. 'Otherwise she'll be sleeping over at her gran's.'

'How do you know that?' asked Will, impressed.

'I know stuff,' said Tom. 'I have my sources.'

'OK, let's hope for the best,' continued Freddie. 'You lot take care of the others. Tom checks up on Hannah; Will, Izzie, and Olly, Xa. Did you get that, Olly?'

'Yeah, yeah,' Olly shouted back.

'Hey, Will,' said Tom, tutting. 'You're so lucky. The gorgeous Izzie! Whoohooo! I just got old Hannah.'

Will chuckled awkwardly.

'Morons,' hissed Izzie. Hannah chewed her lip.

'But how are we supposed to find out if they're at home?' asked Will.

'The phone, dimwit.'

Tom put on a girly voice: 'Hello? This is Beth. Is my darling friend Izzie at home?'

'Exactly,' said Freddie. 'And then you immediately get word to me. Got it? And if Charlie's mum doesn't muck things up for us, we'll meet at my place at nine. My parents are going out tonight. Opera or something.'

'Lucky you,' shouted Olly from below. 'What am I supposed to tell my parents?'

'Tell them that you're sleeping over at my place?' suggested Freddie.

'My parents would *never* let me do that,' said Will. 'I'll have to sneak out. But I'll have to be home by eleven – that's when my dad gets back from work. If he catches me, there'll be . . .'

'Is he still hitting you?' asked Freddie, so quietly that the C.H.I.X. could barely hear him.

'Don't want to talk about it,' mumbled Will.

The treehouse fell silent for a moment.

Then Tom shouted: 'Hey, I think something's biting.' He quickly pulled up his string, but there was nothing on it, except for some dripping pond scum.

'How often do I have to tell you not to yank it out like that?' groaned Will.

'Fishing is stupid anyway,' said Freddie. 'Stupid and boring.'

'You're just saying that because you're the only one who hasn't caught anything,' joked Tom. 'So, we meet at nine at your place. Then we go to the grandma's house. And then what?'

'"And then, and then,"' repeated Freddie, annoyed. 'You'll find out later. The girls haven't found the treasure yet either. So it won't be easy.'

'Well, I'm not looking in that henhouse!' Tom declared. 'Just so we're clear.'

'Me neither,' said Will. 'My granddad says where

there's chickens, there's rats.'

The C.H.I.X. grinned at each other.

Suddenly Olly appeared at the bottom of the ladder. 'I've cracked it!' he shouted to his friends. 'It's an awesome trick. Wait till you see this.' He panted his way up the crooked ladder.

'Hey, you're supposed to be keeping watch,' Freddie barked at him. 'Not playing with your stupid cards.'

'Never mind that,' chuckled Olly, as he hoisted himself on to the platform. A moment later his feet joined the others above the pond. 'What am I keeping watch for? You really think the girls will come here, in their pants, and on foot? Seriously?'

Even Freddie had to laugh.

'Just you wait. You won't be laughing for long,' hissed Charlie, rubbing her nose angrily.

'Check it out. This is the best card trick you'll ever see,' said Olly, excitedly. 'Watch . . .'

'We don't want to see your stupid trick,' jeered Freddie. 'It's lucky that the girls can't hear you. You two *heroes* are afraid of chickens and you can't think of anything but stupid card tricks. I've had enough of this.'

'Shut up,' cried Tom. 'Who stole the girls' clothes? We did, that's who. You've just been sitting here, mouthing off.'

'Then go and find yourself another boss,' roared Freddie, jumping to his feet. 'Or maybe I should find myself another gang.'

'What a bunch of losers,' whispered Izzie.

Will suddenly snorted with laughter. 'Hey, Freddie, you should've seen their faces when we nicked their clothes. It was just like in the movies!'

The C.H.I.X. had to stop themselves rushing out of their hiding place and throwing the Piranhas into the scummy pond there and then. Above their heads, Olly and Tom were nearly falling off the ledge with laughter.

'Don't get too cocky,' grumbled Freddie. 'Even if those girls are as brainless as their chickens.'

'Like all girls,' added Olly.

Hannah and Xa turned as red as toadstools. Charlie clenched her fists. Blotches appeared on Izzie's face and she bit her hand to keep quiet.

'Exactly,' said Tom. 'They're all so dumb.'

'You can talk! Who is it that fancies Izzie then? You even wrote her love notes. Saw them with my own eyes.'

'No!' said Olly. 'What did she say?'

Will was snorting again.

'I just wrote them for a laugh,' said Tom, angrily chucking an empty crisp bag into the water.

'Hey, I told you to stop that,' said Freddie.

'Did he really write you love notes?' Hannah whispered into Izzie's ear.

Izzie nodded. Now there were too many blotches on her face to count.

'Come on,' whispered Charlie. 'We've heard enough. My mum's going to be back at the scrapyard in ten minutes.'

'One thing I don't get,' they heard Will ask. 'This treasure. If we find it, doesn't it belong to the grand-ma?'

'Nah!' answered Freddie. 'Treasure belongs to whoever finds it. Everyone knows that. It's probably stolen stuff anyway.'

'Yeah?' mumbled Will.

The C.H.I.X. crept away as quietly as they had come, their faces set with determination.

Chapter Fourteen

Charlie's mum had to drive her taxi that night.

'I'm sorry,' she said to Charlie. 'But tonight there's a big conference. I can make as much money in one evening as I usually do in a week. And I'll be home tomorrow after school. OK?'

'It's all right, Mum!' said Charlie. 'Xa asked me to sleep over anyway.'

She didn't like lying to her mum, but this time there was no choice. Charlie didn't really expect the Piranhas to find her grandma's treasure – they were far too stupid for that. But the thought of the boys snooping around Gran's house – trampling over the carpets in their scummy trainers, ferreting about in drawers with filthy fingers – made her feel quite sick. No, they had to be stopped, even if that meant having to lie for a change.

COMING SOON
C.H.I.X. BOOK 2

ISBN: 978-1-904442-87-5